Dear Parent:

Congratulations! Your child is taking the first steps on an exciting journey. The destination? Independent reading!

STEP INTO READING® will help your child get there. The program offers five steps to reading success. Each step includes fun stories and colorful art. There are also Step into Reading Sticker Books, Step into Reading Math Readers, Step into Reading Write-In Readers, Step into Reading Phonics Readers, and Step into Reading Phonics First Steps! Boxed Sets—a complete literacy program with something for every child.

Learning to Read, Step by Step!

Ready to Read   Preschool–Kindergarten
• big type and easy words • rhyme and rhythm • picture clues
For children who know the alphabet and are eager to begin reading.

Reading with Help   Preschool–Grade 1
• basic vocabulary • short sentences • simple stories
For children who recognize familiar words and sound out new words with help.

Reading on Your Own   Grades 1–3
• engaging characters • easy-to-follow plots • popular topics
For children who are ready to read on their own.

Reading Paragraphs   Grades 2–3
• challenging vocabulary • short paragraphs • exciting stories
For newly independent readers who read simple sentences with confidence.

Ready for Chapters   Grades 2–4
• chapters • longer paragraphs • full-color art
For children who want to take the plunge into chapter books but still like colorful pictures.

STEP INTO READING® is designed to give every child a successful reading experience. The grade levels are only guides. Children can progress through the steps at their own speed, developing confidence in their reading, no matter what their grade.

Remember, a lifetime love of reading starts with a single step!

For Mom—who showed me how to
look on the bright side.
And for Dad—who showed me
that anything is possible.
—R.T.

Copyright © 2006 by Richard Torrey

All rights reserved. Published in the United States by Random House Children's Books, a division of Random House, Inc., New York.

STEP INTO READING, RANDOM HOUSE, and the Random House colophon are registered trademarks of Random House, Inc.

www.stepintoreading.com
www.randomhouse.com/kids

Educators and librarians, for a variety of teaching tools, visit us at
www.randomhouse.com/teachers

Library of Congress Cataloging-in-Publication Data
Torrey, Rich.
Beans Baker's best shot / by Richard Torrey. — 1st ed.
    p. cm. — (Step into reading. Step 3)
SUMMARY: Beans Baker cannot play in his championship soccer game because his foot is in a cast.
ISBN 0-375-82839-7 (trade) — ISBN 0-375-92839-1 (lib. bdg.)
[1. Soccer—Fiction.] I. Title. II. Series: Step into reading. Step 3 book.
PZ7.T64573Bh 2006 [Fic]—dc22 2005012222

Printed in the United States of America
10 9 8 7 6 5 4 3 2
First Edition

STEP INTO READING®

STEP 3

Beans Baker's Best Shot

by Richard Torrey

Random House · New York

The game was almost over.
The score was tied
with just seconds to play.
The winner would go
to the championship.

Whomp!

Beans passed the ball
to his best friend, Chester,
then raced toward the goal.
Chester passed it back.
Beans kicked with all his might!
GOAL!

"Great pass!" shouted Beans.

"Great shot!" Chester replied.

"Thanks," said Beans.

"Could I get a shot
of the two stars?"
asked Beans' father.

"Aw, Dad!" said Beans.

The championship game
was all Beans and Chester
could think about.

They made plans
in their secret tree house.
"If we win,
let's put our trophies here,"
said Chester.
"Great idea," said Beans.

It was the day before the big game.

Coach Munhall told
Beans and Chester they would be
in the starting lineup.

"Way to go, Chester!" shouted Beans.

"Way to go, Beans!" shouted Chester.

Out on the practice field,

Beans raced for the ball.

Chester raced, too.

They both kicked

at the same time.

Crunch!

"Oops!" said Chester.

"OUCH!" cried Beans.

"I'm sorry," said Chester.

"*Ugh,* I'm okay," groaned Beans.

"We better have it x-rayed,"

said Beans' father.

At the hospital,
Beans and his father
met with Dr. Walt.
"You'll be as good as new
after the cast comes off,"
said Dr. Walt.
"Cast?" cried Beans.

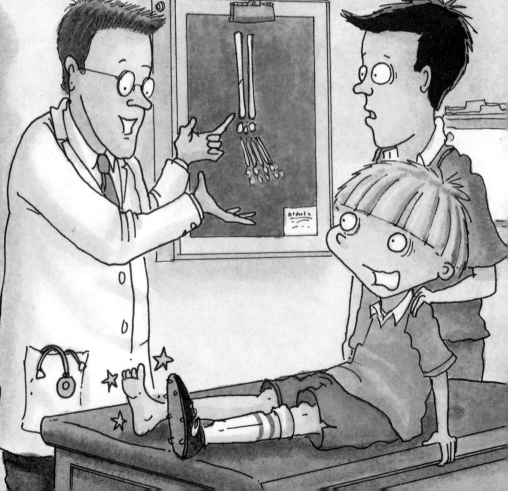

"Your foot has a fracture,"
explained Dr. Walt.
"The cast will help it to heal."
"But I will miss the
championship game!" cried Beans.

Beans' friends were sad
to see him on crutches
the next morning.
They tried to cheer him up.

Chester was too nervous
to talk to Beans.
He hid as his best friend
hobbled past him.

"Everyone has to sign Beans' cast,"
shouted Lindsay.

"It will be our good luck charm
today!"

"Unless Chester signs it," whispered Sheldon. "Then it will be our *bad* luck charm."

"Thanks to you,

Beans can't play," said Sheldon.

"It was an accident!" said Chester.

"I would never hurt Beans.

We're best friends."

"You mean, you *were*

best friends," said Sheldon.

Chester felt terrible.
He couldn't sign
Beans' cast now!

After school, the team
headed to the soccer field.
"Are we ready, Wildcats?"
asked Coach Munhall.
"ROAR!" went the team.
Nobody noticed Chester
sneaking the other way.

22

The fans were arriving.

The other team was on the field.

Soon the big game would start.

"Chester *has* to sign my cast before the game," said Beans. Everyone looked around. But there was no Chester.

"Chester knows the game
is starting," said Molly Mall.
"Where *is* he?"
"I think his feelings are hurt,"
said Russell.

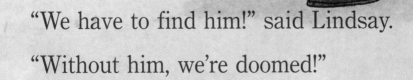

"We have to find him!" said Lindsay.

"Without him, we're doomed!"

"Too bad Chester doesn't have
a cast we could sign," said Sheldon.
"Why don't we sign
a soccer ball for him?"
asked Coach Munhall.
"That would cheer him up."

"Perfect!" said Beans.

Everyone wrote a message
to Chester on the soccer ball.
"How are we going
to give this to Chester?"
asked Molly Mall.
"We don't know where he is."
"Leave that to me," said Beans.

The referee blew his whistle.

The game was about to start!

"Hurry!" said Russell.

"Good luck, Beans," said Molly Mall.

"We're counting on you," said Lindsay.

"I'll give it my best shot!" said Beans.

Beans knew right where to look—
the secret tree house!

"Special delivery for Chester!"
he shouted.

Then Beans took careful aim
and kicked.

WHOMP! The ball flew
right into the tree house.

"Wow!" said Chester.

He read every message
and smiled.

"So you're not mad?" asked Chester.

Beans shook his head.

"But I *will* be if you won't

sign my cast," he said.

Chester scurried down
and signed Beans' cast.
"Best friends?" asked Chester.
"Best friends," said Beans.
"Now come on, there's
a championship game to win!"

Back at the soccer field,
things were not going well
for the Wildcats.
They were behind by two goals.

But when they saw
Beans with Chester,
everyone began to cheer.
"Are you ready to play, Chester?"
asked Coach Munhall.
"I'll give it my best shot!" said Chester.
"Good work, Beans!" the coach said.

The whole team
began to play better
with Chester on the field.
Sheldon scored.
Then Russell scored.
The game was tied!
"It looks like our luck
is changing!" shouted Beans.

With just seconds to play,
Chester passed the ball
to Molly Mall,
then raced toward the goal.
Molly Mall passed it back.
Chester kicked with all his might!

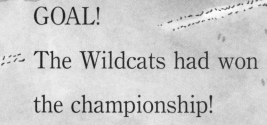

GOAL!

The Wildcats had won

the championship!

Everyone ran onto the field.

They jumped up and down.

They gave each other high fives!

Chester was lifted onto

his teammates' shoulders.

After Coach Munhall handed
out the trophies,
it was time for the team picture.
"Great shot, Chester!" said Beans.
"Your best shot ever!"
"Thanks," said Chester.

"And this is *our* best shot ever!"

said Beans.